THE
THREE
TRICERATOPS
TUFF

THE THREE

Beach Lane Books · New York London Toronto Sydney New Delhi

stephen shaskan

TRICERATOPS TUFF

Once upon a time,
sixty-eight million years ago,
there lived three triceratops brothers
who went by the name of Tuff:
Stanley Tuff, Rufus Tuff, and Bob Tuff.
Food grew scarce for everyone,
so the Tuffs set out to get some grub.

They came upon a valley.
On the other side,
lush vegetation grew—
plenty for everyone.
"Dinner is served!" said Rufus.
"Not so fast," said Bob.
For at the bottom of the valley stood a . . .

TYRANNOSAURUS REX!

"What are we waiting for?" asked Stanley.
"Let's go get that grub!"

And he marched right down into the valley!

Clip,

clomp.

Clip,

clomp.

Clip,

clomp.

"Who's that clip-clomping through my valley?"
roared the T. rex.
"The name is Tuff. Stanley Tuff,
and I'm crossing this valley to get some grub."

"Not so fast, Stanley,"
said the T. rex.
"Dinner is served . . .

... and you're it!"

"But my bigger brother is on his way," said Stanley.
"He'd make a **much** better meal
for someone as mighty as you."

"Then scram, squirt!" said the T. rex,
thinking himself quite lucky.

Next, Rufus Tuff headed down into the valley.

"Who's that clip-clomping through my valley?"
roared the T. rex.
"Uh, the name is Tuff. Rufus Tuff,
and I'm just following my little brother
so I can get some grub."

"Not so fast, Rufus," said the T. rex.
"Dinner is served . . .

"Then take a hike, half-pint!" said the T. rex,
thinking himself even luckier than before.

Next, Bob Tuff headed down into the valley.

CLIP,

CLOMP!

CLIP,

CLOMP!

"Hit the road, Rex!"

Bob served the T. rex such a mighty blow with his tail that he was knocked clear out of the valley and never seen again.

And then, at last,
dinner **was** served...

FOR

For the families and staff of
the Seward Childcare Center

BEACH LANE BOOKS • An imprint of Simon & Schuster Children's Publishing Division • 1230 Avenue of the Americas, New York, New York 10020 • Copyright © 2013 by Stephen Shaskan • All rights reserved, including the right of reproduction in whole or in part in any form. • BEACH LANE BOOKS is a trademark of Simon & Schuster, Inc. • For information about special discounts for bulk purchases, please contact Simon & Schuster Special Sales at 1-866-506-1949 or business@simonandschuster.com. • The Simon & Schuster Speakers Bureau can bring authors to your live event. For more information or to book an event, contact the Simon & Schuster Speakers Bureau at 1-866-248-3049 or visit our website at www .simonspeakers.com. • Book design by Lauren Rille • The text for this book is set in Family Dog •The illustrations for this book are rendered digitally. • Manufactured in China • 0113 SCP • First Edition •10 9 8 7 6 5 4 3 2 1• Library of Congress Cataloging-in-Publication Data • Shaskan, Stephen. • The three triceratops Tuff / Stephen Shaskan.—1st ed. • p. cm. • Summary: On a mission to find some grub, three triceratops brothers must first find a way to outsmart a *Tyrannosaurus rex* with his own dinner plans. • ISBN 978-1-4424-4397-6 (hardcover) • ISBN 978-1-4424-4398-3 (eBook) • [1. Fairy tales. 2. Folklore—Norway.] I. Asbjørnsen, Peter Christen, 1812–1885. Tre bukkene Bruse. II. Title. • PZ8.S3407Th 2013 • 398.2—dc23 • [E] • 2012012475